How It All Began

Fulton Books, Inc.
Meadville, PA

Published by Fulton Books 2021

ISBN 978-1-63860-343-6 (paperback)
ISBN 978-1-63860-344-3 (digital)

Printed in the United States of America

The Adventures of Carly and Charly

How It All Began

CARLY AND CHARLY

Carly

It all began late one morning in August when, all of a sudden, several kittens emerged. One of them was me. And just before that, my twin brother Charly was born. Sure, he's older, but only by thirty minutes. Sometimes I have to remind him that we're almost the same age.

No matter how hard I try, I can't seem to remember how many of my family were born on that fateful day. All I know is that there were two of us. As it was then, it is still.

I can't remember the first few months of our lives. But one day, we found ourselves in a kennel at the Humane Society. The people there were very nice to us. Because Charly and I are twins, we always do everything together.

People often comment on how much we look alike. We met some other kitties, but looking back now, it's all a blur to me. But our bond as twins is unbreakable.

Then one day, Charly and I and a kitten from another family went on a road trip. We three were in a carrier in the front seat of something quite unfamiliar to me. I don't think Charly will admit it, but I'll admit that I was scared. We were moving quickly, and there were

all sorts of new sights and sounds. I didn't know what to make of it, but I knew that as long as we were together, things would be fine.

After I don't know how long–this was before I could tell time–all of a sudden, the moving machine came to a halt. Was this good or bad? Who knew? Should I be happy or sad?

And then there was a voice assuring us that everything would be fine, but I didn't understand English at the time. Sounded like gibberish to me. But her voice was nice. Not much we could do about it anyway. We were still in our carrier after all.

Then we emerged to find a whole new world. I was a little scared, but not Charly. He bounded out of the carrier to check it all out. Not one to miss out on an adventure, I slowly came out of the carrier to join him in checking out the new place. I have to admit it was an impressive space.

Wow...there were food bowls, cat beds, blankets, and toys...and did I mention food bowls? Oh, and there was a litter box right out in the open. Being quite shy, I knew I had to go, but I was reluctant to use the box with everyone watching. What can a shy kitten do to get some privacy around here? Sheesh!

But when you gotta go, you gotta go. And so I did. Then everyone else did too. I'm not one to brag, but I'll take credit for breaking the ice, so to speak. You're welcome.

We were not quite aware of what was what, but we were being fostered, whatever that means. The three of us, Charly and me, and a handsome kitten from another family. The fostering part was important because there was medicine involved. We three all had goopy eyes and wheezy breaths. It's really hard to be your best self with goopy eyes, trust me.

The pink stuff, I think it was pink, didn't taste too bad. But the drops that our guardian put in our eyes were just plain cold. There is a funny feeling when something lands on your eyeball from out of the blue. Notice that I am learning my colors. Thank you.

Charly

I am happy as a clam
Yet for sure, not a clam I am.
Now I'm always warm and dry,
Except for the stuff they put in my eye.
I now know that I love to be a pet
Who knows what I haven't felt yet?
I now understand the meaning of love
It's what I've always been dreaming of.

I spend hours and hours cleaning my paws,
Paying extra special attention to my claws.
And when it's time to eat,
First, I hear the approaching feet.
Oh, happy, happy day,
Food is not far away. (Thank goodness!)

Our guardian is surely great
To land here was a twist of fate.
This place is quite cozy
So my preferred speed is to mosey.
Our toys are all quite clever and fun
And so is lying in the sun.
I really like to sleep and play
And make important plans for my day.

My memories of the kennel are long gone
As we all heal and move along.
I know that I'm happy here with my props
Yes, even with those startling eye drops.
For now, that's the way my life rolls
Okay, as long as I'm closest to the food bowls.

Carly

So you see that we are happy as can be when we found out we will stay here.

The third kitten moved to be in a home of his own. We will surely miss him, and we hope his new mom will kiss him.

For my brother Charly and me, who knows what our future will hold? I do know one thing, being with my brother is pure gold.

Lessons from
How It All Began

Carly

Being together with family is the
most special part of life.
It's the expression of pure love when
people care for us and feed us.
We are so grateful to have a home, a loving
guardian, and especially each other.
Even when things seem scary at first, they
can still work out to be just purrfect.

About the Authors

Carly and Charly are twins who started in life as shelter cats who were fostered and then adopted into a loving home. They wrote this book to share their core messages of hope and love...with a flair for fun and adventure. They are cats, after all.

Carly and Charly have already overcome a lot, and they are planning big things for the future. Together, they are navigating life. They remain optimistic that they can take on any challenges that life throws at them, as long as they have each other. They'd be absolutely thrilled if you joined them on their journey.

They'll never forget where they came from. And as an act of gratitude, they are allocating 75 percent of the net proceeds from this book, and others in this series, to the Humane Society where it all began.

CPSIA information can be obtained
at www.ICGtesting.com
Printed in the USA
LVHW071145061121
702555LV00003B/17

9 781638 603436